A CHAT BEFORE DINNER

MICHAEL KINDSWOOD

ABOUT THIS BOOK

A record of a Zombie's rant about the trials and tribulations of his life as a disrespected member of the Undead.

A Chat Before Dinner is a darkly-humorous 2,600 word short story.

Enjoy the book! After you're done, please come to Michael's website and sign up for his mailing list at http://www.michaelkingswood.com/newsletter-signup/. Guaranteed to be spam free, he uses it to announce new releases and special promotions for his fans.

A CHAT BEFORE DINNER

It's a hard life, being a zombie.

No, really. You try one day finding yourself craving, not that awesome filet from the local steakhouse, but a nice flank cut from the neighbor down the street. Let me tell you, the steakhouse filet tastes much better.

So why not stick with that? Why go the human route?

Believe me, I tried, but there's just something more satisfying about man flesh. I suppose you could say it's an acquired taste.

But not just any hunk of human will do.

At first, I tried just going to the morgue, but that about killed me. Yeah, bad pun I know. But seriously, that cold, dead meat just played havoc with my guts. And if, God forbid, they've already started the embalming process? Formaldehyde is NOT a pleasant taste at all, and it burns going down. Better to starve.

No, fresh warm human is the way to go.

Of course, everyone has their own taste in this matter. This guy I know over in Rock Hills Cemetery loves it really rare. If it ain't still kicking, I don't eat it, he says.

But me, I prefer it more on the medium side. Right on the edge of passing on, but not completely dead yet. It gives the meat a little extra zip, if you know what I mean.

Now, my girl, she won't touch it until it's fully dead. Says she doesn't like it too bloody. I guess I can understand that.

But no one, and I mean no one, will eat it after it's gone totally cold.

Do I feel bad about it? Sure, sometimes. A lot more at first than I do now, of course. Every so often though, I'll be eating some hot broad, and a part of me will realize, hey, she's actually HOT.

Or she would be, if I still looked at humans that way.

I mean really, I'm no pervert here, but I remember how it was back before I changed. Sometimes part of me regrets depriving some human fellow of the pleasure of her company.

It only lasts a second, of course. I mean, you might feel bad for eating a deer or a cow for a short while, but you don't dwell on it. Survival of the fittest, the natural order, right? It's no different with me.

What's that you say? It's NOT part of the natural order? Well, let me get to that in a second.

The other bad part about zombie life is, of course, the accommodations. I mean really. Crypts, sarcophagi, open graves...these are not fun places to hang out.

The vampires though, man, those guys have it made. They've got their own mausoleums, plush felt-lined coffins, human minions and guard dogs.

Do we get any of that? Hell no.

Just try convincing a human that it would be glamorous to get turned into a zombie and see what how he reacts. Being laughed at like that is NOT good for the ego, let me tell you. But somehow those vamps have humans lining up like sheep for a shot at the prize.

Stupid fleshlings don't know what they're missing.

And of course, Dracula and his boys are always rubbing it in our faces too.

I tell you, it's a conspiracy. The man just goes out of his way to keep us zombies down. Well, we're not gonna take it forever. One of these days, the rank and file of the undead world is gonna rise up, and ol' Vlaad will WISH he'd shown us more respect. Just you wait.

But getting back to my point, it gets freaking cold in those places, man. And it's wet. Plus, there's bugs out the wazoo. And sometimes in the wazoo, too. Let me tell you, THAT is uncomfortable. And a bit gross, to be perfectly frank.

Speaking of gross, that brings up another annoying thing about zombie life. It gets really tiresome to have little bits and pieces fall off.

Yeah, yeah, I know. We're walking corpses. We rot. But what you humans don't know is we also grow back. It's this tiring cycle of rot, fall off, grow back. Rot, fall off, grow back. Over and over and over again.

I could accept it if all I did was slowly rot away. Hell, back when I was human that's all I was really doing anyway. It was just on a longer time scale than your typical zombie rot.

But now, I go through a whole set of skin every

week or so, and my other soft tissues, about every month. It makes it really hard to pick up the zombie chicks when your tongue falls out of your mouth.

I lost out on two prime catches that way.

I mean, we all lose parts every day or so. Did I complain when Sheila's ear fell off into my food? Hell no! But man I lose one pound of flesh and she says I'm going to turn into a skeleton if I don't take better care of myself.

You believe that? A skeleton! Those dudes ain't got nothing on me, man!

I tried to tell her that, but she just gave me the finger...literally...and stormed off.

I hear she's with JuJu down by the old dungeon now. That condescending prick. Just cause he was a prize fighter or whatever back before he changed, and managed to stay fast and strong, while the rest of us hobble around all day...

Whatever.

Fortunately, my current girl is more understanding than the others, and I'm very happy with her. She appreciates me for who and what I am.

Which I guess brings me back to your little question. It's appropriate, I guess, since it illustrates the single worst part about being a zombie: having to deal with the constant, unending bigotry from you humans.

Maybe it's just your way of dealing with your inferiority. I guess I can understand that. You are, after all, our prey. It must make you feel insecure.

But really, just because we tend to shamble around doesn't mean we're weaklings. And just because sometimes our vocal chords have rotted out and the only sound we can make is a pathetic groan doesn't mean we're stupid.

Sheesh, my roommate was a PhD, for Christ's sake!

I mean really, if you let him, he'll talk your ear off, literally, about the intricacies of quantum mechanics, and the leading theories on how to merge it with relativity, or some such. I dunno much about all that, but I'm telling you that guy's smart. And he can cook, too.

Look, I understand how stereotypes get started, and that they all have some basis in truth, however small. But seriously folks, would it kill you to sit down and talk with an average zombie BEFORE making a movie about us?

Ok, I guess it would. Probably.

But that's not the point.

I mean, where do you guys *get* this shit? Seriously, brains? Brains? Who the hell goes stumbling around with their arms stretched out in front of them, moaning "brains" all day? And who the hell actually *eats* brains? No one I've ever met.

Really folks, it's called research. It would take all of five minutes to learn this stuff.

But then you guys can't seem to do the minimal research it would take to learn that spy satellites are not in geosynchronous orbit over the United States, or anywhere else for that matter. Do you have any idea how high geosynchronous orbit is? Good luck getting good pictures from there, dude.

And while I'm on the subject, you just can't get real time video, complete with thermal imaging, off them. Neither can any jackass cop just call a Navy Lieutenant to get data from one of these satellites whenever he feels like it, just because he happens to be the bad-ass ex-SEAL she's banging, so he can get a nice deus ex machina assist in solving the case that's stumped him for the last forty-five minutes of prime time television. He especially can't call her from a cell phone and expect to get an answer when she's deep inside CIC on an aircraft carrier.

Way the hell out at sea.

Seriously? Where the hell do you think the cell towers are for that signal? Sheesh, you freaking humans.

See, it's that kind of stupidity and laziness that pisses me off and makes the movies you people try to make about us suck so bad. Really. Do your homework for a change, people!

Wow, I didn't plan to go off on a rant. Sorry about that.

But getting back to it, if all we had to deal with from your racism was bad movies, I wouldn't really complain. I mean, I like a bad zombie flick as much as the next guy. Hell, me and my buds have gotten many a good laugh from Night of the Living Dead (probably for different reasons than you do).

But no, we also have to deal with all those asshole zombie hunter wannabes.

Here's where I get back to the whole natural order bit. And I'm being serious here. Do some cows decide they're going to hunt humans for a change? Some lambs or goats? How about chickens, do they ever come hunting you? No? Ever wondered to ask why?

I'll tell you why: the natural order.

They eat what they eat. You eat them. It's called the food chain, people. I think it's covered in elementary school. So where do you get off thinking it's ok to come hunting us?

What's that? Self defense? Yeah right.

Ok look, if I'm taking a human down, and he turns and whacks me instead, he's a) very very impressive, b) probably not really human, and c) legitimately defending himself.

But that's not what I'm talking about. I'm talking about some jackoff who gets a bunch of gear and comes trying to hunt ME down. How does that become ok and in keeping with the natural plan?

Don't go off on that whole "Zombies aren't part of the natural order" bit. That's totally racist. And also patently untrue from even the most cursory of examinations. There have been zombies for as long as there have been humans. Vampires, werewolves, and walking skeletons too.

But really, don't put those last guys in the same category as the rest of us. They're really quite embarrassingly pathetic, truth be told.

Might as well claim all those guys aren't part of the natural order either. But since they are, you really can't say zombies aren't. Quod erat demonstrandum, my friend.

What? You say they're not natural either? Dude, have you even listened to anything I've been saying for the last few minutes? You really are irretrievably dense aren't you?

But anyway, getting back to these zombie hunters. It would be one thing if they were actually serious, but they're not. And that's the most insulting thing about them: they come completely unprepared.

I suppose maybe they think they're ready to rumble in their minds, tiny though they may be. But I've yet to meet or hear of one who didn't show up looking like he'd taken his cues from the worst of the bad Hollywood zombie flicks. At best. Some of these schmucks show up with garlic and crucifixes, for Christ's sake! I mean, seriously? That shit doesn't even really work on vampires, let alone on us.

Pathetic.

And then you've got the morons who come packing heat. Sometimes they think they're really being clever by loading silver bullets.

Woooo! I'm really scared! Hey jackass, I'm a fricking walking corpse! A lot of good shooting me is going to do you! Might as well hit me with a pillow!

Interestingly enough, this one guy did that a couple weeks back. He actually came the closest to getting away of anyone in the last year. It helped his cause that one of my eyes had rotted out earlier that day, but the pillow was actually quite effective at tripping me up. If he'd been in shape, as opposed to being a blubber butt, he might have made it. But in the end, it didn't matter.

Mmm, that was some nice, tender meat.

Where was I? Oh yes, the douchebags with guns.

I tell you, man, I must have encountered a half dozen guys like that in the last year. Each and every one had the same stupid, confused look on his face when I started eating him, like he couldn't understand how his careful Hollywood research failed him.

You know, I told you before that I don't care for meat that's too rare, but for those idiots, I made an exception.

So what's the right way to kill a zombie then?

Wouldn't you like to know. Who do you think I am, Ernst Stavro Blofeld to your James Bond? I'm not just going to tell you the whole plot, secure in my superiority and the fact that you'll be dead in a few minutes, so what can it hurt.

No, that's something you'll have to learn the hard way. If you get the chance. Which, as I just mentioned, you won't.

So anyway, I've really enjoyed this little chat, but my girl's going to be here in a few minutes, and like I told you she prefers her meat fully dead. So I'm afraid I need to start getting things ready.

What's that?

Oh come on now. You're really just embarrassing yourself. Hell, if you keep it up I'll be embarrassed *for* you.

There's this little thing called meeting your end with dignity, my man. Didn't your dad ever teach you about that? Fighting to the end, not giving the bastards the satisfaction, all that?

Oh, you never met him, huh. Well, sorry about that. If it's any consolation, my folks split up when I was two, so I was never all that close with my dad either.

What are you looking at?

Oh! Hey babe, I didn't hear you come in. Sorry, I'm running a little behind tonight. Dinner will be ready in just a moment.

Can I get you a drink? Ok, well make yourself comfortable.

Quite a looker, eh my man?

Hmmph. Well no offense, but I saw your little squeeze earlier and she's not much to talk about at all. NO meat on those bones. How do you have any fun with a girl like that? Aren't you afraid you'll break her?

Oh well, it's a moot point now, I guess. Better get to it.

Hey, stop squirming! This will hurt a lot less if you just hold still.

MESSAGE FROM THE AUTHOR

Thank you for reading my book. I hope you enjoyed reading it as much as I enjoyed writing it.

Every review helps an author out, so whether you loved this book, hated it, or something in between, please take a minute to tell other readers what you thought. All of the online retailers make it very easy to do, and I would really appreciate it.

Feel free to come say hi at my website or on Facebook. I always enjoy hearing from readers, especially since you all are, collectively, my boss.

I also have a weekly podcast, Story Time With Michael Kingswood, where I read stories and talk through some of the latest goings on in my world. I'd love to see you there.

Thanks again. My best to you and yours.

Warm Regards,
Michael Kingswood

MAILING LIST

If you enjoyed this book and would like word on new releases and special deals from Michael Kingswood, sign up for his newsletter on his website. Guaranteed to be spam-free, you can opt out at any time. And you can rest assured he will not share your information with anyone, for any reason.

https://michaelkingswood.com/newsletter-signup/

Michael Kingswood is 20-year veteran of the US Navy submarine force and a lifelong fan of science fiction and fantasy literature. His work has appeared in numerous collections and anthologies, to include the Fiction River Anthology series from WMG publishing. He holds a bachelors degree in Mechanical Engineering as well as a Master of Engineering Management and a Master of Business Administration. He has four children and currently resides in San Diego.

Find Michael Kingswood online at:

www.michaelkingswood.com

www.facebook.com/michael.kingswood

steemit.com/@michaelkingswood

NOVELLAS

What Lurks Between

The Necromancer's Lair

The Champion

Veritas Morte

STORY COLLECTIONS

Tales Of Adventure #1

Tales Of Adventure #2

Short Story 10-Pack

A Jar Of Mixed Treats

SHORT FICTION

Michael has also published a number of shorter works,
links to which can be found on his website.

www.ingramcontent.com/pod-product-compliance
Lightning Source LLC
Chambersburg PA
CBHW032054180726
48284CB00004B/1342